担子

[下册]

Carrying Load

高山 著

担子
你挑起了希望
你挑满了善良
挑战了人生
挑明了道路
挑起了家的栋梁
挑选了心的模样

作家出版社

目录 CONTENTS

担子／下册／现代诗

寻　梦

背一箩星辉
揽一轮皓月
我踽踽而行

盈一眶热泪
斟一樽清茶
我坦然而去

夜色是我的闺蜜
清风把我抱紧
空空荡荡的躯壳啊
随风摇曳
空无一物

飘逸的长裙
遮挡我前行的视线
隐约的星光
忽暗忽明

天空蓝得发紫
那是梦游的错觉

Pursue My Dream

Carrying a basket of starglow
Embracing a bright moon
I wander and linger

Filled with tears
Poured a cup of tea
I left unperturbed

Night is my close friend
Breeze hugs me tight
The empty shell of my body
Sways in the wind
Hollow

Elegant long skirts
Block my sight
Faint starlight
Flickers

Sky blue blended with violet
Illusion of sleep walk

寻梦

拐一圆方的木杖

踱一围婀娜的身姿

诗人啊

你梦在何方？

寻梦

寻一寸寂寞的墙

觅一缕迷魂的香

野塘的青蛙代我发言

那是我忧郁的心声

缠绵不断

寻梦

寻一盏闪亮的明灯

照耀我消沉的心坎

抹一身耀眼的光环

不、我不要光环

我要继续寻梦

寻梦

那是我心头的忧伤！

往日的彷徨！

2015年夏－北京

Pursue my dream

Take a walking cane

A slender figure

My poet   where does your dream lie

Pursue my dream

Seek a length of isolated wall

Seek a wisp of bewildering incense

Frog in the pond speak for me

Voice of my sad heart

Echoing   lasting

Pursue my dream

Seek a bright light

Lighten up my sinking heart

Surround me with a dazzling halo

Oh no I want no halo

I would rather continue

Pursuing my dream

The mourning of my heart

The confusion of my past

Summer 2015

Beijing

梦中梨花地

哟哒的马蹄
遗落一地的浮尘
繁华背后
沾满油污、堆积如山的烦锁
无处安放

夜幕降临
大地和衣怒躺
舒展着宽广的睡袍
睡袍下面
沉睡着千千万万的虫子
横七竖八、奇形怪状
期待着明天的太阳
太阳的威力
去把他们催赶

夜、依然如故
没有一丝声响、以致
牛鬼蛇神、张牙舞爪
天一亮、即刻
他们即刻消亡

Pear Blossoms in My Dream

The clattering horse hoofs
Restless dust left along the path
Behind the glory
Troubles stained with grease piled up like mountains
Nowhere to put aside

Night fell
Land lay down in anger with clothes on
Extending loose rope
Under which
Thousands of worms were hibernating
Oddly shaped sprawling about
Expecting the sun to rise again
Power of the sun will drive them away

Night the same as before
So soundless that ghosts and monsters
Bare their teeth and open their claws
Once the day breaks
The disappear instantly

然而、忽然
黑漆漆的夜
舒履开一片灰白
灰白慢慢的模糊
模糊出一片混乱
混乱过后沉寂片刻
沉寂出了一片亮丽的梨花地

黑沉沉压抑着
梨花地异常的宁静
宁静出一片秀丽娇影
白如琼玉、娇嫩柔弱
素淡的芳姿飞舞
飞舞出淡雅的清香
清香了一片浪漫

梦中的梨花
梦中的梨花地
有你、有我的身影
婀娜而坚韧
刚强而柔美

梦中的梨花
梦中的梨花地

Yet suddenly
Cold black night spread out a mist of white
Blur into confusion
Followed by a moment of silence
From which a land of pear blossoms rise

Heavy with darkness
Unusually quiet
From the quietness delicate figures show themselves
Pure and tender as jade
Beautifully dancing
Fragrance and elegance
All join in romance

Pear blossoms in my dream
A land of pear blossoms in my dream
Carry the journey of wind and rain
Contain the laurel and glory
Mysterious but depressed
Longing while fearing

Pear blossoms in my dream
A land of pear blossoms in my dream
Cultivating the seed of love
Soothing the wound of affection

承载着风雨兼程
蕴藏着文武衣冠
迷离而忧郁
憧憬而彷徨

梦中的梨花
梦中的梨花地
种育着爱的种子
安抚着多情的伤口
点点滴滴
续续断断
期待着爱的甘露
庄严的洗涤

2014 年秋

Bit by bit

Off and on

Expecting the bath of love

Baptism of solemn

Autumn 2014

味　道

年日如草
岁月如歌
有些味道
虽然逝去已久
依然津津有味
翩翩如初

有些味道
虽然天天沾染着
却早已平淡如水
没有了知觉
好像不曾来过
好像不曾有过

生活
没有了以前的味道
刻木死板
为活而活

朋友
没有了以前的味道

Taste

Days taste like grass
Years sound like songs
Some memories
Long lost
But still worth tasting
Tasty as before

Some tastes
Fade from day after day
Plain as water
Senseless
As if never appeared
As if never experienced

Life
No longer as before
Dull   mechanical   stiff as a poker

Friends
No longer tasty as before
Play the fool   pretend to be insane

斤斤计较
装疯卖傻

恋人
没有了以前的味道
疑神疑鬼
慌慌张张

工作
没有了以前的味道
得过且过
苟且偷生

一切
过得那么快
又过得那么漫长
那么匆忙又那么无奈

我依然如故
蹲在原处、心灵的窝棚
寻找着原来的味道
寻找着

望着时间、飞驰的骏马
杨起远去的灰尘

Lover
No longer as before
Suspicious
Nerve frayed

Work
No longer as before
Muddle through
Keep a mere vegetative existence

Everything passed
So quickly
So slowly
In a hurry   in impotence

I am still myself
Squat where I was   shelter of my soul
Searching for the feeling of the past
Searching on

Watching time flying by like a horse
Stirring dust along the path
Follow my clip clip   horse hoofs
Back to my longing vows and pledges

任由嘚哒的马蹄
带走我曾经的思念
海誓山盟

变了
一切都变了
任由多情的泪水
把我浑身洗涤
点点滴滴
通透淋漓

举目四望
没有看到什么
没有看到
用力呼吸
没有嗅到什么
没有嗅到
尽力舔一舔
只有自己的味道

变了
一切都变了
闭目冥想
没有声音
没有味道

Changed
All are changed
Have my sensitive tears
Washing me all over
Bit by bit
All through

Looking around
Seeing nothing
Nothing
Breathe deeply
Smelling nothing
Nothing
Lick hard
Only my own taste

Changed
All are changed
No sound
No smell
No color
Empty　void

Suddenly I hear myself

没有颜色
空空荡荡

忽然闻到、自己
胸膛跳动的声响
那么深沉
那么执着
那么不曾放弃
孤独而憧憬着
浪漫的日子
迷人的味道
不曾停止

2014 年夏天

Bumping inside

Deep

Strong

Never give up

Longing lonely

For romantic days

Charming smell

Never end

Summer 2014

今夜，我要住进你心房

今夜
我要住进你心房
我害怕寒冷的侵袭
我恐惧饥狼的嚎叫

曾经
迷途于荒野、河畔
颤抖于密林、山丘
呼啸的寒冬
吹碎了我铁的骨头
钢的身躯
海的意志、飘散

散落
只有痴情把我救起
贴合了肌肤
柔弱的气息、奔腾
缓缓流淌的溪水啊
清澈见底
潺潺流淌、今夜
那里、我看见了你

Tonight I Want to Live in Your Heart

To night I want to live in your heart
For fear of the attack of chilly cold
The hungry howling of wolves

Once I strayed in the wild by the river
Shivering at the think forest and hilly dunes
Wuthering winter night
Breaking my bone of steel
Body of iron
Will of the sea scatter

Wandered around
Only infatuation saved me picked me up
Heal my skin
Weak breath start to surge forward
Stream running slow
Pure and clear
Chattering on
Tonight I see you over there

今夜
我要住进你心房
用砖把情围住、把心挂起
砌筑坚实的城墙
坚固而久远
抛下世俗的眼光
宁静而无顾

温柔敦厚的心瓣
一拍一合
把我轻轻抚摸
一波三折爱的春流
把我熔化
熔化的是我孤独的心

今夜
我要住进你心房
忘了今生喧嚣
忘了前世梵吟
得了相思
救了无助
曾经迷茫的羔羊
有了归处
有了栖宿之所

Tonight I want to live in your heart
Surround the affection with bricks hung up my heart
Build solid walls strong and lasting
Ignore the worldly views
Calm and determined

Tender and honest heart valve stroking me
Open and close
Winding spring river of love
Melt me
Melt my lonely heart

Tonight I want to live in your heart
Forget the noise of this world
Forget the promise of prelife
Suffering lovesickness
Saving the helpless
The once stray lamb
Find its home
To stay in peace

今夜以后、以后
长期霸占你心房
霸住、不再疯狂
飘零、流浪

From tonight on

I will occupy your heart

Hold on to it

No more insanity

No longer drifting or wandering

担　子

小时候
偏僻的农村
弯弯曲曲的羊肠草道
一望无际金灿灿稻田

凶猛的水牛边
脆弱的我
单薄的肩膀上、挑着
一副晃悠悠担子

左边是鸡
右边是鸭
绒毛松散叽叽喳喳
嗷嗷待哺

长大了
郊区的小城
零零散散三三二二的人群
时走时停忽左忽右的篷车

Carrying Load

My childhood
At a remote village
Dirt paths winding
Golden wheat fields endless
How weal I was
By side of a strong buffalo
A load swinging
On my bony shoulders

A chicken on the left
A duck on the right
Furry feathers loosened
Chirping and chattering
Dying for food

Growing older
At a small town
A crowd of people
Walking stop and go
With overloaded trucks driving by

灼热的水泥马路上
年少的我
柔软的肩膀上、挑着
一副硬绑绑担子

前面是米
后面是书
摇摇欲坠叮叮咚咚
艰难前行

后来
工作了
诺大的城市
熙熙攘攘红红绿绿的男女
来来往往黄黄白白的轿车

宽广的柏油马路上
成年的我
结实的肩膀上、挑着
一副无形的担子

这边是兄妹
那边是单位
踏踏实实规规矩矩
一丝不苟

The cement road   burning hot
Young as I was
Carrying a hard load
On my soft shoulder

Rice in the front
Books at the back
Shaking   stumbling
Struggling my way forward

Later
I worked in a big city
Noisy with all walks of people   red and green
Busy with all kinds of cars   yellow and white

On a wide asphalt road
I was an adult
Strong shoulders
Carrying shapeless load

Brothers this side
Duty and work that side
With my footsteps steadyfast
Orderly and carefully

再后来
成功了
花花绿绿的大世界
各种各样皮肤东南西北的方言
宏观微观经济古今中外的思想

人生感悟道路上
成熟的我
深沉的肩膀上、挑着
一副梦寐以求的担子

左边是追求
右边是奉献
如履薄冰小心翼翼
无怨无悔

担子
肩膀上的担子
越来越重却又
越来越轻

担子
牵挂的担子
越来越远却又

Still later

With my dream achieved

In a bigger world

Meet people of all colors and different languages

Thinking about economy macro and micro

Reflecting the past and the present the Chinese and the western

On the road of life

I am now mature

With my dream load

On my tough shoulders

Pursuit on the left

Dedication on the right

Walk with caution as if on thin ice

But without regrets

Load

On my shoulders

Heavier and heavier

At the same time

Lighter and lighter

Load

越来越近

担子
你挑起了希望
你挑满了善良
挑战了人生
挑明了道路
挑起了家的栋梁
挑选了心的模样

担子
可爱又深沉的担子
我愿一生
把你形影不离的挑在肩上
与你并肩作战

2014年秋

Of concern

Farther and farther

Yet nearer and nearer

From load

I learn about

Hope

Kindness

Challenge in life

Way ahead

With a family to support

With a role model to follow

Load

Lovely and deep

I am willing to carry you all my life

Fight my way on

Side by side

Autumn 2014

绿荫下的女子

我又遇到了
那绿荫下的女子
曾经的风雨飘摇
曾经的爱恨情仇
千年前的微笑
醉倒了草地的诗人

朗朗的读书声
唤醒了多少迷茫
迷茫的花丛中
闪烁着萤火虫的纤光

桌子
敲响了胜利的前奏
前奏中夹杂着美丽的梳妆
镜子下诗的对白
一副相思的模样

夜、侵占了白天
白天灼热的熔岩
熔岩下面

The Girl in The Shade of Trees

I met the girl again
In the shade of trees
The once wind and rain
The once love and hatred
A smile as if a thousand years ago
Struck the poet on the lawn

The sound of reading
Awaken many lost souls
Amidst the hazy flowers
The glow of fireflies
Flickering

Desks
Ring the prelude of victory
Mixed with pretty dressing and making-up
Poetic dialogue
The mirror
Reflected a look of love-sickness
Night occupied day
Day burn the mass of lava

是小鸟的天堂

又遇到了
那绿荫下的女子
娇小的身躯
撑起了天的重量
绘画出水的形状
丈量着大海的浅深

夜、偷走了一切喧嚣
遗忘一角的安宁
书院的架子上
摆放着耶稣的日记
日记的后页
记载着仿佛

又遇到了
那绿荫下的女子
一脸的娇嫩
满头的光亮
又一次
醉倒了草地的诗人

2014 年秋

Under which
Lies a heaven of birds

I met the girl again
In the shade of trees
Delicate figure
Support the weight of heaven
Painting the shape of water
Measuring the depth of sea

Night steal all the noise
Leaving only a quiet corner
On the bookshelf
Sat the journal of Jesus Christ
On the back page
Was recorded ------

I met the girl again
In the shade of trees
A budding flower
With the glow of sunshine over her head
Struck the poet on the lawn
Once again

Autumn 2014

人生是一场错过

凛冽的寒冬
吹落了颤抖的枝头
飘洒的尘沙
飞坠出满屋的金黄
袅袅婷婷的吹烟
缓缓爬行、一圈一圈
叮咚的驼铃
带走了整夜的温存
一串一串
浅浅淡淡的印迹
刻录下苍海的沧桑
弯曲盘旋的沙丘、
起伏不断，飘散
飘散出的，那是人生
人生，酗意的人生
是一场错过
错过了青春
错过了美丽
错过了初潮的羞嫩
错过了秋川的奔流
人生，忐忑的人生

Life is a Scene of Missing

Chilly winter
Blowing off the shaking sand and dust
From the branches
Rest on the floor like a spread of gold
Smoke from the chimney
Rising like slim and supple lady
Steady up   round after round
Bell of the camel jingle jingle
Taking away the warmth of a whole night
String after string
Deep or shallow footprints
Carved the changes of times
Winding sand dunes
Waving   flowing
Just like life
Life lingering in drinking
Is a scene of missing
Missing the young
Missing the beautiful
Missing the shyness of first sign of menstruation
Missing the torrent of autumn tide

是一场错过
错过了微风的轻吟
错过了细雨的抚触
人生，纠结的人生
是一场错过
错过了窗前的深拥
错过了月下的相凝
人生，刻木的人生
是一场错过
错过了多情的表白
错过了魂灵的回响
只有、只能
种下了满头的银丝
丢下了整脸的皱纹
怀着蹒跚的步伐
追逐弓残的背影
远去。人生
是一场错过
最痛、最苦
是错过了你！
有如那远远的高山！

2014 年冬

Life passing in wondering

Is a scene of missing

Missing the chanting of breeze

Missing the stroking of drizzle

Life agonizing in dilemma

Is a scene of missing

Missing the big embrace by the window

Missing the deep gaze under the moonlight

Life imprinting on the bone

Is a scene of missing

Missing affectionate confession

Missing resounding of soul

Leaving only

Only the grey hair all over my head

Wrinkles all over my face

With stumbling steps

Chasing the bent back figure

In the distance

Life

Is a scene of missing

The most painful the most tearing

Is missing you

Like the distant high mountain

Winter 2014

岁月静好

五月的初夏
清风袭脸
电闪雷庭
漫山遍野的翠绿
沉沦于蛙叫蝉鸣间

我沉醉于书林词海
行间字里
横冲直撞、忽闻
一目十行
捷步争先、看见了
雪峰皓月
仙草绵绵
霓虹闪烁的宫殿
还有那金色的门天

仙女驾驭着驼铃
琼楼玉宇、似梦非梦
袅袅婷婷
祥云飘逸着凡世
万仞千峰、似山非山

Happy Quiet Hours

Early summer of May
Breeze strokes my face
Lightning strikes the yard
The fresh green of moutains and fields
Sink in the frog croaking and cicada chirping

I am indulged in phraise and verses
Charging between words   listening
Read through ten lines at a glance
Pace up and see
The bright moon above snow peak
Holy plants waving
A palace with neon lights flickering around
And golden gate to the heaven

Fairies riding on camels
A house of jade and crystal as if in dream
Delicate clouds
Floating over the earthly world
A thousand peaks seem unreal
As if in sleep

若休若眠

心在万物上、却又
身在万灵中
以最初的心
寻找最远的路、不停
三世前的禅定
万年后的梵行

我携跨越千年
的沧桑岁月
掩盖日暮天涯
的云舒云卷
浮生若梦的物是人非
缘薄情悭
似水无痕

我将晨钟暮鼓
盛装你的倾世温柔
我欲涅 重生
诠释有你的似水流年

阳光温热
百花争鲜
尘世喧嚣

My mind goes beyond everything
While my body among all beings
Seek the fartherest path
With the original intention
Persistantly
In predestined deep meditaton
And Buddhist practice thousands of years from now

Cossing the many centuries
Interchanges of sea and land
Covering the many dusks till the end of the world
Clouds coiling and extending
Short lives in the dreamy world
Things remain the same but people different
Thin both in luck and love
Leaving no trace like on the surface of river

I keep your tenderness
In dawn bells and dusk drums
I would resurrect in nirvana
To prove the flowing years with you

All flowers bloom
In warm sunshine

日夜不宁

岁月静好
你若不来
我怎敢老去
休闲天地间

2015 年夏夜

Worldly clamour and chaos

Endless

Happy quiet hours

Without your company

How can I grow old

And wonder around in leisure

On a summer night of 2015

我的母亲

我的母亲
是个农村小姑娘
早年失母
幼年无父
孤苦伶仃
无依无靠

我的母亲
是个富人家丫环
日夜劳作
衣不蔽体
食不果腹

我的母亲、长大了
亭亭玉立
忧伤的双眸里
注满了憧憬和希望
贫困没有吓倒她
却吓倒了饥寒

我的母亲

My Mother

My mother
Was a girl in the country
Who lost her parents
At a young age
Poor and lonely
With nobody to rely on

My mother
Worked as a servant
In a rich family
Day and night
Dressed in raggs
Left in hunger

My mother gew into a pretty lady
Her sad eyes
Were filled with hope
And expectation
Poverty didn’t beat her
Nor did she give in to cold and hunger

My mother

是个幸运女人
贫瘠的土地上
偏僻落后的小山村
竟遇到了她的白马王子
魁梧的父亲大人
从此、不再孤单
有了依靠的肩膀

我的母亲
是个农村妇女
勤勤恳恳
踏踏实实
起早贪黑
不慌不忙
肥沃了土壤
翠绿了河山

我的母亲
是个文盲
却能感悟孔孟之道
教子有方
古今思想
日月星辰

谆谆教诲

Was lucky to meet her Mr Right
In the poor land
Of a backward village
Who was my father
Tall and strong
A shoulder to rely on
My mohter was no longer lonely

My mohter
Is a woman in the country
Hardworking
Steady and sure
Early to rise late to rest
Following the natural course
Plough and sow in spring
Good harvest in autumn

Ill educated
As Mother is
She understands Confucius and Mencius
Taught us thoughts of the past and present
Knowledge of nature
In her own way

With her love and patience

语重心长
我们如饥似渴的兄弟姐妹
都是她的学生
人生的课堂上
不敢偷懒

我的母亲
是个独守老人
她的孩子和丈夫
奋斗在遥远的大街小巷
日夜兼程、风雨无挡

创造着财富与尊严
回馈着社会与发展
体弱多病的她
却选择独自一人
鸦雀无声
独守空房

我的母亲
是个慈祥的老人
左邻右舍的大中小事
都是她的忧伤
家长里短的烦恼纠结
都由她过问

Care and devotion
We kids learned
Like a sponge longing for water
Daren't idle
In the school of life

My mother
Lives alone
When her kids and husband
Went far away to study and work
From dawn till dusk
Whether windy or rainy

When we create wealth and dignity
For the development of society
She chooses to live alone
Old and weak
In her quiet old house
All by herself

My mother
Is warmhearted
Concern about the neighbours
Incidents whether big or small
Help them out of troubles

她吞下了苦水
却开心把果子交给了别人

我的母亲
是一条静静流淌的河
静静流淌
是一首悠扬美妙的歌
字字珠玑

我的母亲
是一面不辞劳苦旗帜
缓缓升起
是一缕傲雪无暇的梅
独自生香

我的母亲
你的孩子、斗志昂扬
奋斗在大江南北
富饶的土地上
坚强不屈、坚韧不拔
因为、宽怀着你的思想
梦寐着你的榜样

我的母亲
你不屈不挠的精神

Take in the bitter

Bring about happiness

My mohter

Is like a quietly flowing river

Flowing quietly

Like a beautiful song

With words of crystal ripples

My mohter

Is an example of diligence

Rising

A plum blossom against cold and snow

Fragrant in itself

My mohter

Your kids work in high spirits

On fertile lands

Of different parts of the world

Strong willed

Persistent

As we all hold on to your dream

Following your example

My mother

洒满了山海江河
鱼儿也为之感动
化为力量、潜能
自强不息、逆水飞身

母亲、我的母亲
我以哥哥的风范
带领顽皮弟弟
娇羞的妹妹
生生世世
万载千秋、追随

跟随着你、跟上
永远投胎你家里
做你的孩子
孝顺的孩儿
乖巧伶俐的学生

母亲、我美丽的母亲
娇艳又可爱
母亲、我善良的母亲
平凡而伟大、母亲
我们都爱你、爱你
母亲！快乐、母亲！

2015 年夏－母亲节

You never gives in to hardship and difficulty

Your spirit is spreading and reflected on mountains and rivers

The fish is also touched

And try their best to swim

Against storms and high waves

Mother my mother

As your eldest son

I would lead my naughty brother

And shy sister

To follow you

Life after life

We will follow you keep up with you

In recarnation

Always be your famliy

Filial children

Obedient and clever students

Mohter my beautiful mothter

Pretty and lovely

Mohter my kind mother

Common but great

We all love you Mother

May you happy! Mother

On Mother's Day of 2015

我们相约去偷海

电闪雷鸣
狂风乱作
我们
还是相约去偷海

沙漠的丘沙在飞舞着
着实想渴死人类
我们
还是相约去偷海

手握得紧紧的
你断把的勺子
碰到了
我陈旧缺脚的木桶
我们相约去偷海

那里
太美妙
那里
太自由
那里

Agreed to Fish Secretly

Lightning   Thundering
Stormy
Still
We agreed to fish secretly

Sand in the desert swirling
Trying to dry humans
Still
We agreed to fish secretly

Hand held tight
Your spoon with handle broken
Struck on my bucket with one corner missing
Still
We agreed to fish secretly

There is
Beautiful scene
There is
Much freedom
There is

才是我们的家

电闪雷鸣
荆棘丛生
或许
有毁灭的痛
我们
还是相约去偷海

2014 年春

Our real home

Lightning   thundering

Thistles and thorns

Perhaps

Pain of destruction

Still

We agreed to fish secretly

Spring 2014

输给了时间

我们
都输给了时间
它穿着华丽的羽绒
张牙舞爪着
嚎叫着

它手中锋利的锯齿
把我们千丝万缕的
海誓山盟粘成的思念
一小段一小段的锯走
最后
剩下一只空壳
飞舞着

它把一个个虚伪
按入蜜糖缸里，凉干
然后
剥去层层粘稠的外衣
剩余一只
跳动的，赤裸裸的
肮脏的心

Lost to Time

We all
Lost to time
It is howling
Baring its fangs and opening its claws
Wearing fancy feathers

Sharp saw tooth
Cut off all the ties
Of missing each other
Stuck together with vows and pledges

Leaving finally
An empty shell
Floating

It presses one hypocrisy after another
Into honey jar
Dry up
And peel away the sticky coat
Leaving only
A beating naked

它
分离着骨头与肉
理所当然的
没有报酬与感觉
夜里
它一个一个吞噬着
人类，美丽的梦
不知不觉的，可怕

原来
时间才是宇宙的主宰
我们
都是猎物，微小的
不足挂齿

2014 年春

Dirty heart

It separates the bone and flesh
Without naturally reward or feeling
At night
It swallows the beautiful dreams of humans
One by one
Before they know it
Terrible

Time turns out
To be the master
Of universe
We humans
Are but its prey
Too small to mention

Spring of 2014

说好春天来看我

下雪了
雪融了
春天近了
记住说好春天来看我

隔远了
平淡了
活着活着就老了
记住说好春天来看我

哭过了
笑过了
肉体与灵魂升华了
记住说好春天来看我

春天
我的世界
你的世界
相融
说好了

Promised to Come and See Me in Spring

Snow fell
Snow melt
Spring approached
Remember you promised to come to see me in spring

Distance lengthened
Relationship faded
We get older as we live on
Remember you promised to some and see me in spring

Cried
Laughed
Flesh and soul ascended
Remember you promised to come and see in spring

Spring
My world
Your world
Integrated
Promised

说好春天来看我
我在
海边等你
去年已搭好了帐篷
凛冽的夜晚
说好了

2014 年春

Promised to come and see me in spring

I will be waiting

For you by the sea

Tent was put up last year

On a chilly night

You promised

Spring 2014

爱

爱、是真爱
纠缠着春夏秋冬
冷落了花草树木

爱、是嗔爱
记恨了云雨？
颠覆了山河？

爱、是什么？
花童告诉你
仙桃告诉你

花一样的美
桃一样的香

2015 年夏

Love

Love　true love
Tangling four seasons
Leaving trees and flowers behind

Love　annoying love
Showing anger about cloud and rain
Upturning the mountain and river

Love　what is love
Flower kids can tell you
Peach fairy can tell you

Beautiful as flowers
Fragrant as peaches

Summer 2015

跟着感觉走

跟着感觉走
白云悠悠、小山沟
珍禽异兽、狮子头
才渡长江口
又横鹦鹉洲
人间何处寄忧愁

跟着感觉走
跟着黄河游
千里江河一杯酒
万年黄历一轻舟

才出唐宗
又至今朝
时间甚比人风流
随风随雨
任天任地
君复何求？

笑观沧海
静看杰豪

Follow My Heart

Follow my heart
White clouds drifting
Over the small valley
Rare birds and animals lion head
Just passing the Yangtze River
Now crossing the Parrot Island
Where can I leave my sorrow
In this vast world

Follow my heart
Down the Yellow River
A thousand miles traveling
While drinking a glass of wine
Ten thousand years spending
On a light boat

Tang Dynasty then
Modern era now
Time seems more carefree than man
Windy or rainy
Depend on the fate

昨夜邻家盛宴
可有曹操？

跟着感觉走
日行千里
夜榻琼楼
对酒当歌知音何处
抚弦鼓乐夜读诗书

跟着感觉走
不畏丛林宽百里
无惧郊野出恶虎
昂首挺胸、银河漫步
从不心孤、从不影独

跟着感觉走
轻飘飘
尽逍遥
庄子遇上大鹏鸟
谁家公子逗天娇
聚雀桥、弄舞腰
绿柳飞、枝千条

跟着感觉走
黄梁一梦终归醒

Wheat else am I pursuing ?

Watching the misty sea with a smile
Looking at the heroes in quietness
The grand feast at next door neighbour
Was Cao Cao invited ?

Follow my heart
Cover a thousand miles a day
Stay over night at a fairy house
Drinking accompanied with songs
Playing music rather than reading poems

Follow my heart
Fearing not the deep forest
Or wild beasts
Hold my head high
As if strolling on the Milky Way
Never feel lonely at heart
Always find a partner to go with

Follow my heart
Flowing
Floating
Zhuangzi meeting a hawk

不想天亮
又见门响
隔壁梁伯叫话
诗人何去？

唉、美梦
真好！

2014 年秋

A young man teasing a heavenly beauty

Gather at Que Qiao (bridge formed by magpies)
Dancing elegantly
Like young willows stretching
A thousand delicate branches

Follow my heart
Finally awake from a fantasy dream
Not want the day to break
When there came a knock
On the door
It is Mr. Liang next door calling
"Time to go to work."

Autumn 2014

失　眠

昨夜
失眠了
彻彻底底的
眼睁睁的望着天花

没有一丝睡意
直至把黑夜
望成满天的星斗
闪闪烁烁

昨夜
失眠了
不由分说无可抵挡
毫无预兆无可救药
辗转反侧心神不宁

没有一丝睡意
好像一头
被活活烧烤着的肥猪
无奈又好奇

Sleepless

Sleepless
Lat night
Totally   thoroughly
Staring at the ceiling blankly
Not a sense of sleep
Staring until darkness turning
Into a sky covered with stars
Twinkling

Sleepless
Last night
Unreasonable   unavoidable
Unpredictable   incurable
Tossing   turning back and forth
Restless
Like a fat pig toasted alive
Helpless but curious

Sleepless
Last night
Bright days with breezes and showers

昨夜
失眠了
历历在目和风丽雨
波涛汹涌激情澎湃
似曾相识心有灵犀

没有一丝睡意
以至飘飘浮浮若醉若仙
原来热血沸腾
连人带被
摔到了地板上

昨夜
失眠了
不知过了
多少年月多少春秋
阳光穿透了娇羞的纱窗
灼热了我懒散光滑的肌肤

终于坐起
心口忽然隐隐作痛
浑身无力冷汗淋漓
步如浮云身如飞絮
此时此刻
世界与我无关

So real like yesterday

Passionate as roaring waves

Familiar and consonant as our hearts are linked

Not a sense of sleep

Flying like a fairy

I am actually

So exited as to be thrown onto the floor

Together with the quilt

Sleepless

Last night

So many years passed

Before I know it

Before the sun shines through my shy window

And warm my idle silky skin

Sit up

A dull pain at heart

Weak and wet with cold sweat

Treading on clouds

Light as willow catkins

Now

This world is miles away

昨夜
失眠了
一切因为忧伤的你
你走进了我的骨头
你走进了我的细胞

干枯荒芜的心田里
如此真实
如此恐怖
如此无止无休

如果让我选择
夜幕降临
明天还要失眠
因为可以想你、梦你
梦里梦外
都有你！

2014年秋

Sleepless

Last night

All because of your sadness

You enter my bones

My cells

My dry deserted heart

So lifelike

So breathtaking

So lasting

If I could choose

I would rather be sleepless

Tomorrow

When night falls again

Then I could think of you   dreaming of you

Always you

Whether inside or

Outside my dream

Autumn 2014

学　堂

小时候
遥远的地方
一望无际的田野
鸟语花香
男耕女织

一不大不小的鱼塘边
几间破旧的泥土瓦房
那是我的故乡

年小的我
被父母丢进了学堂
弱小的身子
迷迷茫茫

长高了
不远的粟米地
一条弯弯曲曲的泥巴路

大人小孩
高矮肥瘦

School

I spent my childhood
At a distant country
Endless land
Birds singing   flowers fragrant
Men labouring in the fields
Women weaving cloth

My hometown
Is beside a small fish pond
A few shabby clay houses

At a young age
I was put into the school
Weak and small
Lost

Growing taller
A winding muddy path
A corn field not far away

Adults and kids

一处河边的玉米地
几处崭新的砖房

那是我的摇篮
懂事的我
乖乖的走进了学堂
慌慌张张

后来
千里之外
一色彩斑斓的城市
人头攒动
车水马龙

一泉水叮咚的清溪边
一幢幢整整齐齐楼房
那是我人生的训练场

饥渴的我
梦寐以求的
走进了学堂
匆匆忙忙

再后来
大千世界

Either tall or short fat or thin
Field by the river
Several new brick houses

That's where I grew up
More sensible I became
Obediently walked into the school
Full of fear and confusion

Later
A thousand miles away
A colorful city
Crowded with people
And traffic

A chattering stream
Rows of tidy houses
My training ground for life

Thirsty for knowledge
I entered my dream school
In a hurry

Still later
In this boundless world

大大小小的城市
远远近近的国度
形形色色的建筑
新新旧旧的书院

百花齐放
日夜兼程
那是我知识的寻觅地
灵魂深处的召唤声

成熟的我
沾沾自喜的
走进了学堂
坦坦荡荡

学堂
你是我储备精神的
粮仓
你是我放飞理想的
起程
你是我升华灵魂的
洗礼
你是我查阅古今的
书典

Big or small cities
Far or near countries
All sorts of buildings
New or old schools

All flowers in full bloom
Traveling night and day
To my paradise of knowledge
Call from the depth of heart

Mature now I am
Pleased with myself
Proudly walk into the school

A place
Where I equip my self
With spiritual food
Runway for flying my dream
Baptism for my soul elevation
Classic books for me to explore the past and present

School
Contains
Naive and lovely kids
Strong and promising teenagers

学堂
包容着
天真可爱的孩童
血气方刚的少年
雄心勃勃的青年
功成名就的壮年
鹤发童颜的老年

都是你徒儿

学堂
空空如也
却又人才济济
默默无闻
却又百家争鸣

学堂
我愿一生
不曾远离！

2014 年秋
北大

Ambitious youths

Successful middle age

Old age still young at heart

We are all your students

School

Empty

But full of talents

Quiet

But full of divergent voices

School

I wish to be close to you

All my life

Autumn 2014

Beijing University

秋　思

月落星沉
烟柳斜、秋雾重
独上小楼空倚栏
静思陈事暗消魂

红蓼渡头红
鸥迹沙成行
千山万水不曾游
万般惆怅向谁诉

不语含颦楚桥边
几回愁煞钓鱼郎
秋已暮、霜满树
梦归禁城神鼓
独掩珠帘泪无数

秋日长、秋草黄
画梁燕去远宫墙
玉箫无声响
鸾镜掩、人休妆
山月不知诗人事

Meditation of Autumn

The moon sets   the stars descend
Misty willow slanting
Autumn fog hang low
Ascending the pagoda   rely on the railing
Heart sinking in mediation of the past

Meisn render the ferry red
Shadow of seagulls reflect on the sand
With a thousand miles yet to travel
Who will share my melancholy

Standing quietly by the Chu bridge frowning
Leaving the man fishing worried now and then
Autumn deepened   trees frosty
Dream back drums of the Forbidden City
Pulling down the curtain   weeping alone

Autumn long   grass yellow
Swallows flying from the painted beams
Beyond the palace walls
Jade flute soundless

水风空飘落庭花

坐看流水暗叹息
罗袂湿斑泪滴横

2014 年秋

Mirror with the mystical bird is covered

Lady not wanting to make up

The moon rising from the mountain knows not the poet's heart

Wind blowing over the river sees the falling flowers

Sighing quietly at the running water

Silk shirt stained with overflowing tears

Autumn 2014

回　家

从未出家
何为回家

2014 年春夜

Homebound

Never leave home to be a monk

How can I go back home

Spring 2014

朦胧夜色

夜深
独坐、听蛙鸣
风静、雨停
树青青

心空空
梦盈盈
千古愁怀、有谁明？

今生醉
来世情
但求有共声

汹涌激情何处去？
酗情海啸变山形
天无涯角海无边
有谁听？

Misty Night

Deep night
Sit alone listening to the frogs croaking
Wind quiet rain stops
Trees fresh green

Heart empty
Dreams crowding
Sorrows of ancient times   who to share

Drunk this life
Love for the next
Wish to have much in common

Where has my surging passion gone
Rolling waves of passion has frozen into mountain
Sky without edge and sea without end
Who is listening

你是一只开心的小鸟

你是一只开心的小鸟
自由浪漫
任意飞翔

我是一只笨重的企鹅
幽然伫立
暗然伤神

纵然指挥千军万马
呼云唤雨
依然忧伤

有朝一日
愿意跟你流浪
天涯地角
丢掉忧伤

寻找欢腾、日夜喜沾沾
不再牵肠
共喜同欢

You Are a Happy Little Bird

You are a happy little bird
Free and romantic
Flying unrestrained

I am a clumsy big penguin
Stand alone
Deep in gloom

Even with a thousand soldiers and horses to command
Summon wind and call for rain
Still sad and down

Some day
I will roam around with you
Every corner of the world
To relieve my sadness

Seek joy and fun delighted night and day
No more troubling
Only happiness shared

今、冷了吗

今、冷了吗？
一切都会经过狂热与冰冷
曾经的夏天
曾经的狂野

今、冷了吗？
包括爱情
执着的追寻
沾沾自喜的心情

今、冷了吗？
金钱、地位
名誉、追求

今、冷了吗？
难道、一切都冷了
跟随气侯的变化
还是时间的推迟

今、冷了吗？
包括阿诺方舟

My Dear Is It Cold Now

My dear is it cold now
Everything will go from hot to cold
The past summer
The past craze

My dear is it cold now
So it is with love
Constant pursuit
Self contented joy

My dear is it cold now
Fortune social status
Fame aspiration

My dear is it cold now
So everything is cold
With the change of weather
Or the elapse of time

My dear is it cold now
Including Noah's Ark

包括童年的歌谣
包括热气腾腾的包子
包括你、我！

Nursery rhyme

Steaming hot dumplings

Including you and me

卢浮宫之夜

我在阅历着世界
翻看着各地的课本
东西南北，地球的两端
和腹部
看到了战争
听到了强盗锣鼓
和他们引以为荣的战利品
懦弱与强悍
沉思了许久
终于，知道答案
我懂了，知道该怎办
废墟！

A Night at the Louvre

I am reading the world
Turning the pages of text books
From east to west   north to south   both poles of the globe
And the hinterland
I see wars
Hear the gongs and drums of the bandits
And the spoils they esteem as an honor
Weak and strong
Lost in thought for long
I finally come with an answer
I know what to do
Ruins

等

等，等你的出现
等，等适当的时机
等，等上帝赐予我们
相遇的门票
美丽的邂逅

等，大地温暖的时候
鸟语花香、蝶蜂飞舞
我们相吻
等，等我们心智成熟
义无反顾、无牵无挂

等，等我们世界只有彼此
因为、其他已透明
其他已无谓

等，梦中也欢笑
在那山间、在那河畔
等待你，等
等你的出现！

Wait

Wait wait for you to come
Wait wait for the right time
Wait wait for God to bless us with tickets
For a beautiful chance meeting

Wait for the land to warm up
With birds singing flowers fragrant
Butterflies and bees dancing
We will kiss
Wait wait for us to be mature both heart and brain
With no turning back with no ties and cares

Wait wait for there to be a world of us two
As the rest is clear
The rest doesn't matter

Wait to laugh even in dream
In the mountain by the river
Wait wait for you to come

十里银滩

孤帆点点
涛声阵阵
白云片片
踱影双双

海儿蓝蓝
思絮飘飘
隔岸迢迢
鸥飞对对

银沙腻腻
赤足羞羞
千里江河万里景
百年人生千年梦

涛声依旧声声意
晨风拂袖寸寸心

Ten Miles of White Sands

Sails dot the sea
Waves succeeding
White clouds in patches
Lovers walking side by side

Sea water blue
Thoughts swift
The other bank distant
Seagulls flying in pairs

White sand fine
Bare feet shy
Endless scenes along the thousand rivers
Dream of a thousand years in a lifetime

Sound of waves as before sending messages
Morning breeze sway sleeves each bit of my heart

啼声归雪

海清云淡风浅
浪涛声声
疾风紧紧

孤帆万里影
思心阵阵
春心隐隐

君不知
天涯地角飘浮泪
椰林静立寂寞心

思往昔、寸草真
愿作比翼双飞鸟
满天飞月
啼声归雪

Birdsong Immersed in Snow

Clear sea thin cloud wind slight
Waves chasing each other
Wind in flurries

A lonely sail against miles of blue sea
Missing thoughts in waves
Longing heart faint

My friend do you know
After shedding tears at every edge and corner of the earth
I am standing quiet in coconut trees with a lonely heart

Think of the past every blade of grass resemble my true love
Wishing us to be two birds flying side by side
Moonlight brighten up the whole sky
Birdsong immersed in the snow

朋友、别走

朋友、别走
你脚下的路
还很漫长、让我
与你陪伴
与你分享

朋友、别走
记得那风雨飘摇的夜晚
记得那缈无人烟的沙滩
拐伤了的脚步
左右为难、一声多情的问候
解决了无数纠缠

朋友、别走
记得那酒、那千年的甘霖
穿透了喉咙、烤热了衣裳
跳起了唐宋的宫舞
响起了北朝的琴弦
若仙、若我
色彩斑斓

My Friend Don’t Go

Don’t go my friend
There is long way ahead
Let me keep you company
Share the journey with you

Don’t go my friend
Do you remember the night of wind and rain
On a deserted sand
I sprained my ankle
Stranded A caring greeting
Cleared many a trouble

Don’t go my friend
Do you remember the wine like the rain after a long draught
went down the throat heated the clothes
We danced as in the palace of Tang and Song Dynasties
Played the music from Northern Dynasty
Feeling like fairies
Colorful sleeves waving

朋友、别走
深山有你的印记
大海有你的泳妆
戈壁滩上、有你迷茫的身影
野狼在郊外嚎叫
你可曾听到声响

朋友
是困难的拐杖
是成功的助燃
是平静的无语
是天涯的咫尺

朋友
人生的舞台、你
尽情的表演、我
在台下、为你高声呐喊
拍碎了手掌、也心甘情愿

朋友、别走
让我把你跟上
看看后面是否有狼
看看后面无限风光
有时、恶狗也疯狂
容易受伤

Don't go　my friend
Your footprints remain in the deep mountains
Your postures stay in the seas
Your misty shadows reflect in Gebi desert
Can you still hear wild the wolves
Howling　out of town

My friend　you are
My walking cane in difficulty
My accelerant for success
Quietness at peaceful moments
Closeness of the uttermost of the world

My friend
On the stage of life　you
Act to your heart's content　I
Cheer and collapse for you below the stage
Till my hands hurt　willingly

Don't go　my friend
Let me follow you　watching out to see
Whether there are wolves behind
Whether there are boundless views behind
Sometimes evil dogs can be furious
You may get injured

朋友、别走
回头看看
后面已泪波奔腾！
回头看看
大地已枯黄沧桑！

朋友、别走
你脚下的路
还很漫长、让我
与你陪伴
与你分享！

2014 年秋夜

Don't go　my friend

Looking back

Eyes are welling with tears

Looking back

The land is withering

Don't go　my friend

There is a long way ahead

Let me keep you company

Share the journey with you

An autumn night of 2014

遗　憾

儿时
清翠欲滴的野竹林
满地黄叶的泥土地
大人、都提犁带锄
牵牛赶马、去了

剩下、年幼的我
和蹦蹦跳跳的小伙伴们
偷偷摸摸的玩着过家家
左看看、右望望
遗憾没有亲吻年幼的新娘

后来
长出了稀拉的胡子
冒出了骄狂的喉结
声音沙沙作响、虎虎生威
同乡的阿娇、隔村的阿桥

窈窕婀娜、步伐轻盈
羞涩的我、情窦泛滥
头不敢提、眼不敢睁

Regrets

I spent my childhood
In the green and luxuriant bamboo woods
Yellow leaves fallen on the dirt road
Adults were either laboring in the fields
Ploughing and hoeing　or driving oxen and horses

Leaving me with my playmates　jumping and bouncing
Playing house secretly
Peeking this way and that
Regretting that there was no bride to kiss

Later　I began to grow beard
Proud and flimsy when Adam's apple appeared
Voice husky and hoarse　imposing and vigorous
Ah Jiao in the same town　Ah Qiao in the neighbouring villiage

How slim and slender and light-footed they were
How shy I was　flooded with first love
Lowering my head　avoiding their eyes
Fearing that I would be heated and melted

生怕被烤熟了、熔化了
遗憾没有看清她们的模样

再后来
拉上了天窗
成了老爸成了大人
早出晚归奔波劳累
油盐酱醋人情世故

忘了兴趣、丢了理想
旧了琴棋、灰了画廊
遗憾没有重拾年少的志向

遗憾
侵占着我、纠缠着
还有、一切的一切
点点滴滴、断断续续
如春雨绵绵秋雨细细
如纤光袅袅隐隐约约
却挥之不去思之即来

遗憾
我要把你深深埋藏
我要把你无情抛弃
我不要你、我要你远离

Regretting that I didn't see their faces clearly

Still later
I got married and had kids
Left home early in the morning
Returned late at night   rushing around
Occupied with daily routine   worldly affairs

Forgot interests   rejected ideals
Neglecting my guitar and chess
Leaving my art studio in dust
Regretting not returning to my previous dream

Regrets seized me
Tangled me
Everything   bit by bits
On and off
Like spring rain autumn rain drizzling drizzling
Like thin light   dim and faint
Curling and waving
Haunting   emerging whenever I think of them

Regrets
I will bury you deep
I will abandon you ruthlessly

要你、回到那荒芜人烟
天涯海角、宇宙爆发地

明天、明天开始
我要周游世界
我要登高望远
我要远渡重洋
我要飞上太空

明天、明天开始
我要吟诗煮酒、品茶
我要泼墨疾书、摹画
我要扬名海外、天涯
我要通古知今、当下

明天、明天开始
我不再妒忌潘安
我不再暗恋貂蝉
我不再同情织女
我不再羡慕牛郎

明天、明天开始
我要向花问好
我要向水煽情
我要望望天的模样

I don't want you   I will keep you away
Throwing you back to the uninhabited
Far corners of the world where the Big Bang took place

Tomorrow   from tomorrow on
I will travel around the world
I will climb high mountains and look into the distance
I will cross the oceans and seas
I will fly into out space

Tomorrow   from tomorrow on
I will warm wine chant poems and taste tea
Paint and write and copy classical art works
I will make my name known all over   even the end of the earth
I will learn about the past and the present knowledge

Tomorrow   from tomorrow on
I will no longer envy the handsome Pan An
No longer love the pretty Diao Chan in secret
No longer sympathize Weaving Girl   the fairy from heaven
No longer admire Niu Lang   the cowboy

我要舔舔地的甘甜

明天、明天开始
不再孤独、不再忧伤
不再彷徨、不再胆颤
面对碧浪白云
放歌旷野群山、转而
对小鸟点头
对老牛低弹

从此
不再遗憾
夜夜笙歌、与星共舞
日日疯狂、与河同奔
把遗憾远远抛弃！
把遗憾深深埋藏！

2014 年秋夜

Tomorrow   from tomorrow on
I will greet flowers
I will show my love to water
I will look up to the sky
I will smell and lick the sweet land

Tomorrow   from tomorrow on
I will no longer be sad and lonely
No longer hesitate or fear
Facing the blue sea waves and white clouds
Sing aloud in the wild plain and turn to
Nod at the birds and play the lute to a cow

From now on
No more regrets
Night after night   music and dance
Crazy day after day   racing with the river
Keeping the regrets far away
Keeping the regrets down below

An autumn night of 2014

什么是快乐

世人

无识

无从知晓

What Is Happiness

Nobody in the world

Knows

From nowhere

沙　滩

一片白茫茫
粒粒寂寞
一脚踩去
四分五裂
陷了一地
体无完尸

Sands

Boundless whiteness

Each grain of sand is solitude

Step on

Splashing and splitting

Step down

Into pieces

恶　魔

世间的恶魔
是你自己
不能战胜自己

Evil

The biggest evil

Is yourself

One you can't defeat

冷落是罪

违法
是罪
人刻的花纹

原来
冷落
是祸首

2014 年春夜

Negligence

It's a crime
To violate laws
Artificial patterns

The arch criminal
Turns out to be
Negligence

On a spring night of 2014

裙子与袖子的偶遇

夏天来了
裙子花枝招展的
在草丛中游荡
一会儿东、一会儿西
满山遍野都是裙子的身影

青蜓来了
袖子追逐着飞舞的蝴蝶
五颜六色的翅膀
一会儿飞、一会儿停
大江南北都是袖子的脚印

夜半的一鸣春雷
颤醒了沉睡的裙子和袖子
游离开横七竖八初雷的缝隙
她们听到爱的吟弹
坦荡且熟悉
低沉又销魂

片刻
裙子爱上了袖子

Chance Meeting of Skirt and Sleeve

Summer came
Skirt hung around in the grass
Like flowering branches
Here one moment
There the next moment
Leaving her shadows all over the fields

Dragonfly came
Sleeve chased the flying butterfly
Colorful wings
Hovering one moment
Resting the next moment
Leaving his footprints across the land

Spring thunder at midnight
Awoke the Skirt and Sleeve from deep sleep
Drifting away from the zigzag cracks of the lightning
They heard the chanting music of love
Clear and familiar
Deep and ravishing

袖子恋上了裙子
柔弱的裙子抚触着袖子的肩
高傲的袖子拥抱着裙子的魂

从此
世间多了一道七彩的彩虹
群山雨后、嫩绿的春笋
破土出一道道亮丽的光芒
永不凋谢
永不消沉

2015 年夏

In a moment

Skirt fell in love with Sleeve

Sleeve fell in love with Skirt

Tender Skirt soothed the Sleeve's shoulder

Proud Sleeve held the Skirt's soul

Since then

There is an extra rainbow in this world

Soft spring bamboo sprouts

After the rain in the mountains

Spring our rays of bright light

Never fade

Never sink

Summer of 2015

人间那点事

宇宙咆哮着
怒吼道
谁在兴风作浪
暗渡陈仓

太阳自转着
不敢吱声
地球低下头
默默无言

光阴虎视着光明
那点光亮
那点光亮
怎么那么渺小

黑洞俯视着银河
我懒得理你
去吧

ThoseLittle Worldly Affairs

The universe roars

In anger

Who is raising winds and waves

Advance secretly by an unknown path

The sun rotates

Keeping silent

The earth lowers its head

Remaining wordless

Time looks at light fiercely as a tiger

That bit of light

That bit of light

Why so weak

Blackhole overlooks the Milky Way

---I don't feel like talking

Just go

天轻语
人间的那点事儿
有事？

2015 年夏

Heaven whispers

---The little worldly affairs

Are there any ?

Summer of 2015

他为和平而来

——记孔子和平奖组委会主席谯达摩先生

他来了
他为和平而来
两袖清风
笑容可掬

化身达摩的尊躯
踏着第三条道路
披荆斩棘
所向披靡
潇洒而来

他来了
他为和平而来
崎岖的小道
曲折迷离
高矮的山丘
参差不齐
他赤足而来

饥鹰高空盘旋

He Comes for Peace

—On Mr. Gautama, chairperson of Confucius Peace Award Committee

He has come
For the great cause of peace
An official honest and upright
Radiate with kind smiles

Like the saint Siddhattha Gautama
Traveling on the third way
Blazed a way through brambles and thistles
Overcome what he encountered
Natural and elegant

He has come
For the great cause of peace
Winding paths
Twists and turns
Mountains and hills
Ups and downs
He came barefooted

Hungry hawks hovering overhead

虎视眈眈
他豪迈而来
如风如电
如蛟如蟒

他来了
他为和平而来
带着老子的叮嘱
捧着孔子《论语》
携着耶稣的日记
风风火火
日夜兼程

还有释迦牟尼的禅语
穆罕默德的精言
一丝不苟
步步莲花

他来了
他为和平而来
他用沧桑的双手
点亮了智慧的圣灯
人类文明的五大智慧之巅
闪耀登场
仗放光芒

Tigers and lions staring
He came brave and heroic
Like wind and lightning
Like a flood dragon and python

He has come
For the great cause of peace
With the exhortations of Confucius
Holding The Analects
Carrying Journals of Jesus Christ
After the manner of wind blowing and fire spreading
Traveling night and day

Together with Zen Sayings of Sakyamuni
Mottos of Mohammed
Conscientious and meticulous
Every footstep makes a lily grow

He has come
For the great cause of peace
With his experienced hands
Light up the holy lamp of wisdom
Five peaks of human civilizations
Ascend in glory
Cast a thousand beams

他来了
点灯、点灯、点灯
一传十、十传百、百传万
普天同庆
和平之火
处处飞扬

那光亮
那孔子和平奖的春雷
驱散了阴霾
传播了光明
弘扬了传统
承载了国粹

他来了
他为和平而来
他来了
他赤足而来
他来了
他踏着第三条道路而来

他来了
他为和平而来

2015 年夏夜

He has come

Lamp lamp   lamp

From one to ten ten to a hundred and then a thousand

The whole world joins in the jubilation

Flames of peace

Glaring everywhere

The light

Spring thunder of Confucius Peace Award

Drive away the dark clouds

Pass on the brightness

Promote the tradition

Carry the essence of a nation

He has come

For the sake of peace

He has come

Barefooted

He has come

Traveling on the third way

He has come

For the great cause of peace

On a summer night of 2015

我想逃

我想逃
逃离喧哗的闹市
闹市的嘈杂

我想逃
逃离世俗的眼光
眼光的杀戮

频繁的追赶
耗尽我躯壳的潜能
虚无的幻想
吸附我灵魂的力量

忧伤的遗憾
煮熟我童年的梦想
梦想的尽头
是一叶破旧的陈秋

我追寻时光的脚步
步步惊魂

I Want to Run Away

I want to run away
From the busy city
The chaos of busy city

I want to run away
From the mundance
The eyes that can kill

Constant chase
Exhaust the potential of my shell
Futile daydreams
Suck the strength of my soul

Sand regret
Spoil my childhood dream
End of the dream
Is but a shabby past autumn

I follow the steps of time
Startling by each step

我追逐繁华的片段
段段纠心

人生的绳索
捆绑了我飞翔的翅膀
繁忙的枷锁
钩住了我狂野的春心

我想逃
向往南山的青翠
流连北海的波澜
滚滚的红尘
是我马蹄留下的梦

我想逃
憧憬桃园的花蜜
馋嘴夏娃的禁果
隆隆的雷声
是我心头的荡漾

我想逃
逃回儿时的梦
赤裸真诚
我想逃
逃离现实的城

I chase the passages of bustling
With each passage heartending

Ropes of life
Tie up my wings
Chains of business
Hook my wild heart for love

I want to run away
Longing for the fresh green bamboo woods on South Mountain
Lingering around the waves and ripples of North Sea
Billowing Red Dust
Dreams left by my horse hoofs

I want to run away
Hungry for the honey of peach orchard
The forbidden fruit of greedy Eva
Looming thunders
Reverberation of my heart's tide

I want to run away
Back to dream of my childhood
Bare and sincere
I want to run away

虚无缥缈

我想逃!

2015 年夏

From the city of reality

Void

I want to run away

Summer of 2015

雾　霾

大地
披上了皇帝的新装
迷糊、羞涩
怒不可当、又无力呻吟

偷偷的
忍受着、被羞辱的日子
百鸟归巢、万物开春
却没有春的模样
它们睡了

山河哭泣、鸦雀无声
时不时
传来妖孽的声音
恐怖而荒唐
没人吱声

雾霾
夺走了明亮、山川
吸干了万物灵秀
抹黑了太阳

Smog

The land has put on
The Emperor's New Clothes
Confused shy
Furious yet too weak to give a groan

Secretly
Bear the insulting days
All birds back to their nests all creatures ready to welcome spring
But no spring appears
It is still asleep

Mountain and river weep
Crows and sparrows silenced
Now and then
There comes the voice of evildoers
Horrible and absurd
Nobody speaks

Smog
Takes away the bright scenery

谁的杰作
上帝？去吧！
是人类的疯狂

2014年春
北京机场、雾霾

Dries up the beauty of all

Saddens the sun

Whose masterpiece is it

God?　No

It’s the insanity of humans

Spring of 2014

At Beijing airport in smog

一群鸡和鸦

滚滚朦胧处
蛙声四起、人欢马叫
天昏地暗、日月无光

熊猫背着恐龙偷欢
猫头鹰搂着野猪亲吻
癞蛤蟆藏进了冰箱赖床

伏羲无言
女娲无语
隔岸观火

捣蛋的地瓜
满屋的腥味
逐层逐层的剥皮
还有过街的小老鼠

一群狂妄的蜜蜂
千枪万箭
穿透了脆弱的白纸
血肉模糊

A Flock of Chickens and Crows

Amidst billowing mist
Sound the frogs croaking
People bustling and horses neighing
A murky sky over a dark earth
Both the sun and the moon lost their brightness

The panda seeks pleasure behind the dinosaur
The owl kisses the hog
Toads hide themselves in the frige
Reluctant to get up

The first man Fu Xi is speechless
The first woman Nv Wa keeps silent
Watch the fire from the other bank

Naughty sweet potatoes
Fishy smell fills the house
Peel the skin
Layer by layer
Also a rat crossing the street

树林急了
山川怒了
谁在敲锣打鼓
兴风作浪
淹没了我家的小屋

蓦然回首
滚滚朦胧处
一群鸡和鸦
群魔乱舞

2014 年秋

A swarm of cocky bees
Pierce the fragile white paper
With thousands of spears and arrows
Crushed in a mess of flesh and blood

The forest is left worried
The mountain and river angry
Who is beating gongs and drums
Raise winds and waves
Flooding my small house

Looking back I suddenly see
A flock of chickens and crows
Dancing wildly
Amidst the billowing mist

Autumn of 2014

饥　饿

寒风凛冽
群山料峭
光秃秃的树枝叉处
摇晃着几个
孤单单的鸟窝

漆黑处、阴阳怪气
幽幽传来两捆
摇摇晃晃的、蓝光
阴森而柔弱
冷得可怕

一只残弱的羊头
在蓝光面前缓缓渡过
惊慌失措、颤抖哀鸣
如盆中菜、刀下死鬼

蓝光没有停留
继续前进、探索徘徊
它不杀微弱之辈
专吃流星、狂妄之徒

Hunger

Winds sharp
Mountains chilly
Between some bare branches
Several lonely nests are shaking

Ink dark oddly
Comes two bunches of blue light
Flickering
Ghostly pale
Scarily cold

A weak goat head
Passing slowly before the blue light
Panic shivering plaintive cry
Like dishes on the table
Men before the executioner

Blue light moves on
Exploring and lingering
It never kills the sick and weak
Feed especially on the tasty bodies of

美味的躯体

虽然颓废
满肚饥肠
甚至听到锣鼓的声音
从胃部传出

蓝光忽然一闪
黯然熄灭
万籁俱寂

随之
阴森处
缓缓走出一妙龄少女
如风雨忧柔
如梦幻缥缈

远处传来
赖床的背影

梦醒了
听到鸟的声音
还有花儿的味道

2014年春
北大

Shooting stars and arrogant fellows

Though decadent

Starving

The stomach sounds

Even like gongs and drums beating

In a flash

The blue light disappears

Into total silence

Then there appears a young girl

Walking from the gloomy darkness

Tender and depressed like breeze and rain

Ethereal like a dream

From the distance

A back figure of someone attached to the bed

Awake

Into a world of birds chirping

And fragrance of flowers

Spring of 2014

At Beijing University

疲 惫

颤抖的躯壳
拖着消沉的头颅
一步一步
醉醉醒醒
忐忑徘徊着

邻家的狗
叫个不停、或许
异常伤心
找不到寄存心脏的盒子
悲愤哀伤

孤寂的夜
蚕食着他一寸寸的良知
可耻而无能
嗜血如刀的恶魔
践踏着人类

星星与月亮
哭了
被放错了地方

Fatigue

A shivering body
Dragging the lowering head
Step by step
Half drunk
Half awake

Restless hesitate

The dog next door
Keeps barking
Heart broken
Finding no box to keep my heart
Sad and angered

Solitary night
Gnaws his conscience bit by bit
Shamed and incapable
Blood sucking monsters
Are torturing humans

Stars and the moon

应该在天上、怎么
掉下了人间

疲惫
平静去哪了
谁偷走了安祥
善良的人类
怎么混入了牲畜

2014 秋

Are weeping

Misplaced on the earth

Rather than in the sky

Fatigue

Where is my serenity

Who has stolen my peace

Kind humans

Why do they mingle in the livestock

Autumn 2014

流浪的小鸟

我是一只
流浪的小鸟
虽然
没有孔雀华丽的羽毛
也没有子规啼血的歌喉

但
依然早起
从这枝头
飞到那枝尾
看尽繁花听尽喧哗

依然
不敢早睡
生怕
错过了大地美丽的时刻
瞬间的永恒

我
从不言语
因为不敢

A Vagrant Little Bird

A vagrant little bird
I am
Without peacock's feather
Nor the cuckoo's voice
Whose blood drops and turns into azalea

But I still
Get up early
Fly from one treetop
To another
Seeing all the flowers
Hearing all the uproars

But I still
Dare not sleep early
Fearing that
I would miss the beautiful moments of the land
The eternity in an instant

I
Never speak

因为不想
破坏美丽的自然风光

我是一只
流浪的小鸟
从这枝头飞到那树脚
从不言语
依然

2014 年秋

Because I dare not

Want not

To ruin the natural beauty

A vagrant little bird

I am

Flying from one treetop

To another

Silent

Still

Autumn 2014

孤　独

他来了
无声无响、安静淋漓
他脱光所有衣服
滑溜溜的
跟鱼混在一起
在海里翔游

龙王没有理会他
龙王未成年的女儿
送给他甜美的午餐
虾兵蟹将
全被他煮熟了

他摇滚着
坚实的翅膀
翻山越岭
潜入曲折的河流
泪腺满满的

穿梭于三界间
时而宫廷

Solitude

Here he comes
Silent quiet as if he has fallen into pieces
He takes off all his clothes
Naked
Swims in the sea
Amidst the fish

Dragon king doesn't let him be
Dragon king's teenager daughter brings him delicious meals
Shrimp soldiers and crab marshials are all cooked by him

He spreads his strong wings
Over mountains and dunes
Dives into the winding rivers
Eyes welled with tears

Travels between three worlds
Now the royal court
Then the earthly world
Next the hell

时而人世
还有地狱
徘徊、忐忑

他捏着
柿子的肚子
柔弱而怜悯
稍一出力
便流出汁来

他提着
老鼠的胆子
小心翼翼、左顾右盼
着实像个毛贼
浑身颤抖

他昨夜偷了
丘比特的神箭
没有弓箭手和敌人
呆呆的坐着
等太阳起床把他烤死

孤独
可怜的孤鸟
荒弃在孤野

Hesitating　Restless

He holds the stomach
Of a persimmon
Soft and pitiful
A little more effort
And juice will come out

He lifts the gall
Of a rat
Cautious　looking about
Just like a thief
Shivering all over

He stole the arrow
Of Cubit last night
Sits idly
Without the archman or rivals
Wait for the sun to get up and roast him to death

Solitude
Pitiful isolated island
Deserted in the wild
The beast inside him is dormant
The evil inside him is hatching

有兽性沉浸着
有邪恶孵化着
着实可怕

2014年春

Frightening

Spring 2014

声　音

她来了
婀娜多姿
带着风夹着雨微笑着
披着彩虹

初春的嫩绿
沾满了柔弱的气息
夜雨、点点滴滴
飘渺迷离

她来了
昨天夜里
鸡鸣鸟叫、还有蛙声
醉了春的美丽

篱笆在等她
梦了一地
孔雀也凑热闹
还有楚王的舞池
光彩迷离

Sound

She comes
Slender and elegant
Smiling mixed with wind and rain
Covered with rainbow
Fresh green of early spring
Tinted with tenderness
Night rain   dribs and drabs
Wispy and dreamy

She comes
Last night
Chickens crow   birds chirp   frogs croak
Drunk in the beauty of spring

The fence is waiting for her
With dreams scattered over the ground
The peacock joins in the noisiness too
And the dancing floor of the Kingdom of Chu Dynasty
Splendid

All is ready

准备着
六宫粉黛
准备着
文武百官、牛鬼蛇神
还有李白杜甫魂灵

山珍海味、百乐交集
陪随着古曲琴弦
传来了
声音

原来
是天籁
醉了一池
满庭泪声
无休无止

2014 年春

Beauties from the six harems

Officials and offers   ghosts and monsters

And the souls of poets Li Bai and Du Fu

Table delicacies from land and sea   all pleasures mingled

Accompanied by classical music from ancient zither

Comes

The sound

The sound of nature

Everyone gets obsessed

Weeps fill the courtyard

Endless

Spring of 2014

声　音

粗糙、沉浸
大海的潮水
淹没了城墙
毒如蛇蝎
放任

恐怖的黑暗
吞下了黎明
山的轮廓
碎了

嘈杂、放荡
叫花子的街上
游浪着舞女、低俗
贫民区的枯井
干涩开裂

粗暴、强蛮
寒冬的积雪
压抑了艳丽的孤梅
少了皓月

Sound

Coarse deep
The tidal sea
Flooded the city walls
Unbound
Poisonous as snake and scorpion

Horrible darkness
Swallow the dawn
Outline of the mountain
Broken

Noisy dissolute
Beggars on the streets
Dancing girls vulgar
Dried well in the slum
Cracked

Rude and insolent
Accumulated snow from winter
Constrain the pretty lonely plum blossom
No bright moon

嘈杂
恐怖的声音
碎了心、断了弦
乱了人间

2014 年春

Noisy

Horrible sound

Break the hearts   break the strings

Leaving the world in chaos

Spring of 2014

淫　雨

她来了
昨夜三更
婀娜着撒娇着
泪水飞了一地
江南那块柔弱的布席
淹水了

她来了
树木都哭泣着
一身的泪水湿漉漉的
鸟儿也怒了
谁昨夜搞垮它的家

她
想来就来
想去就去
午夜的窗外
可能有她娇柔的身影
她来了

淫雨

Excessive Rain

She came
At midnight
Graceful blushing
Tears splashed all over
The soft cloth matting from the south of Yangtze River
Was flooded

She came
Trees wept
Wet in tears
Birds got angry
Their nests were ruined last night

She
Comes and goes
As she likes
Out of the window at midnight
There may appear her delicate figure
She comes
Excessive rain
You have kept me waiting long

你令我久等了
那枯涩的心田
早已消失
去了梦中

2014 年春

My dry heart

Has disappeared

Into my dream

Spring 2014

游　离

蛇与青蛙
一个在满载荷香的塘中游荡
一个在飞蛾群舞的稻田穿梭
他们约定
看谁更快乐

暴雨来了
遍地浮萍
万河满溢
自然荷塘与稻田也淹没了

蛇与青蛙上了同一块树叶
巨大的船舶
随波逐浪、从此
踏上了飘逸的旅途

谁也不知道他们要去
谁也不知道他们将去
何方

2014 年夏天

Drift Away

A snake and a frog
One swims in a pond fragranced with lotus flowers
The other shuttling in a rice paddy with moths flying over
They make a bet
To see who is happier

Storm comes
Duckweeds scatter
All rivers flooded
Both pond and rice paddy disappear

The snake and the frog
Climb on the same leaf
A hug boat for them
Following the tides and waves
From now on
They are a journey   drifting
Nobody knows where they want to go
Nobody knows where they will go

Spring 2014

天边的那一片云

你是天边的那一片云
时而出现
时而飘走
永远没有踪影

你是天边的那一片云
不曾驻足
不曾悲伤
不知飘去何方

云啊
可否告诉我
天有多大
地有多宽
曾经的爱有多疯狂

为何
总飘来飘去
难道世上还有
挥不去的忧伤？

2014 年夏天

The Cloud Over The Horizon

You are the cloud
Over the horizon
Now appear
Then disappear
Leaving no shadow

You are the cloud
Over the horizon
Never linger
Never regret
Knowing not where you are floating

Please cloud
Can you tell me
How big the sky is
How wide the earth is
How crazy the love once was

Why are you floating
Back and forth
Is there sorrow in the world
That you can't forget?

Summer 2014

心　蛇

太阳
猛烈的烤我
他不知道
我早已无心无肺

月亮
疯狂的唤我
她不知道
我早已无情无义

只有冬天
我才出行
因为我是
那不愿冬眠的蛇

2014 年夏天

The Snake Inside Me

The sun
Is beating on me
Without knowing
I am already a hollow man

The moon
Is appealing to me
Without knowing
I am ruthless　heartless

Only in winter
I go out
As I am
A snake unwilling to hibernate

Summer 2014

红　夜

昨夜、夜里
寻幽忘了愁
玩水游山荡悠悠
散步银滩晚
濯足观鱼沟

消寒避暑好去处
瞻星望月中秋前
一支红酒
四圆秋饼
试茶尝酒又一天

问前人古圣
对画诵经
咏歌鼓琴
倚竹抚松远眺
佳人何处、缈缈生烟
焚香莳花多时
未见忘愁
心依孤

Scarlet Night

Last night
I was exploring the mysterious world
Forgetting my sorrow
Traveling with pleasure
Wandering along the silver sand beach
Bathing my feet by the brook

A resort for both winter and summer
Admire the moon and stars around mid-autumn
Red wine
Mooncake
Taste tea and wine   day after day
Inquire about the saints and scholars in old times
Mediate before ancient paintings and read sutras
Singing   chanting   playing music
Look into the distance leaning on bamboo or touch pine trees
Where is my beloved girl an elegant figure in the mist
Burning incense   bury flowers
Still I cannot forget my sorrow
Still I am lonely at heart

随缘慰亲
习业为善
布施为乐
漱泉赏雪听雨
阅书临帖荡舟
高卧静坐俯瞰
心随云飞
无止无休，

人生百十载
何患风雨
何患喜忧
疏朋熟友
山姑市婆
稀人落客
悲欢离合
得失高低
比之宇宙
微如尘埃
莫伤怀

暂且对酒当歌
观颜笑语
醉几何
喜比忧多

Follow my fate   comfort my beloved
Devoted to learning and doing good deeds
Willing to donate and help others
Drink spring water   appreciate snow   listen to the rain
Reading   practice calligraphy after a model   rowing a boat
Sleep in reclusion   sit in meditation   over looking
Follow the cloud
Forever
Scores of years in one's life
Weather rain or shine
Joy or sorrow
Close or distanced friend
Relatives in the city or countryside
Deserted or isolated
Separations and returns
Gain or lose   up and down
Like universe
Like dust
Never sad or worried

Just sing while drinking/enjoy life while you can
Laughers and smiles
Drunk with no idea of time passing
Joy more than sorrow

忘所过

逐长河

妥。

2014年夏夜

Forget the past

Follow the long river of history

Just right

A summer night of 2014

江南夏夜

波渺渺
水悠悠
江南夏夜惹人愁

杨柳依依
芳草萋萋
恨相见来迟
无何花落去
累果挂满枝

洞庭归客晚
江畔逢故人
不知来者因
只言行路难

王孙游不归
何况布衣裳
千帆过尽东流水
幽幽花城盼君回

谁在舟上

A Summer Night in The South of Yangtze River

Rolling waves
Misty waters
Summer night in the south of Yangtze River inspires sorrow

Willows sweeping
Green grass weeping
Regret late meeting
Can't help flowers falling
Though fruits hanging heavy from branches

Guests stay late at Dongting mountain
Old friends reunite by the lake
Knowing not why they come
Talking about the hardship on the way

Noble young men linger on his trip
Let alone ordinary people
A thousand sails pass on the east bound river
Remote flower city is expecting you

欢颜笑脸轻轻语？
一寸相思千肠断
欲言又止
原来梦里、唏嘘
朦胧随风逐云去
无踪无影谁人知
满脸泪滴

2014 年夏夜

Who is on the boat

Whispers with happy similes

Missing thoughts break the heart

Want to speak but hesitate

It is but a dream   sighing

Follow the wind   chase the cloud

Not knowing where the shadows disappear into

Tears pour down both my cheeks

Summer night 2014

你，要走了吗?

天凉了
地冷了
东西南北、融合了
闷热的夏天溜走了

荔枝红过了
龙眼熟过了
中秋踱来了
你，要走了吗？

青春逃跑了
激情安静了
理解沉默了
亮丽褪色了

老子、庄子、孔子
却谈笑来了
你，要走了吗？

美味尝尽了
天涯荡遍了

Are You Leaving

Weather cooled
Land frosted
Places on the earth become similar
Sultry summer slips away

Litchi turned red
Logan ripen

Mid-autumn stroll near
Are you really leaving

Youth escaped
Passion quieted down
Understanding silenced
Brightness faded

Laotzu   Zhuangzi   Confucius
Started talking and laughing
Are you really leaving

All delicacy tasted

孔雀开屏了
喜怒哀乐了

同道中人
却姗姗来迟了
你，要走了吗?

襁褓长大了
童真遗忘了
少年壮志了
风华正茂了

丘比特的神箭
却又射来了
你，要走了吗?

风，吹动着门铃
却听到脚步的声音
平静带着缓慢
无奈陪着不舍

雨，打骂着门槛
却听到满院的笑语
纯洁参着欢快
憧憬沾着凄美

All landscapes traveled
Peacocks displayed the feathers
All feelings Experienced

People of the same ideal
Come last
Are you really leaving

Babies grown up
Children's simplicity forgot
Youth's will strengthened
Life bloomed

Cupid fired another arrow
At me
Are you really leaving

Wind sound the wind chime
Steps approached
Calm but slow
Helpless yet lingering

Rain beat the doorsill
Laughers in the courtyard came
Purity blended with cheers

夜深了
人静了
梦醉了
你，要走了吗?

愿
岁末
人群中
有你的身影
在寻觅着我
孤独而受伤的心

你，要走了吗?

2014 年秋夜

Longing combined with sadness

Night deepened
People quieted
Dream drunken
Are you really leaving

Wishing
At the end of the year
You are among the crowd
Looking for me
Lonely and hurt

Are you still leaving

Autumn 2014

古书奇谈

春秋繁露
世说新语
大摆筵席
论语

老子、庄子、孔子、孟子
墨子、荀子、列子、孙子
八子齐歌，悠扬起伏

还有
鬼谷子、韩非子
公孙龙子、淮南子
渡江途中、沉迷风景
晏子不知时日
忘了春秋
严重缺席

银河闪烁
百鸟群舞
幽香的庭院里、桌台上
堆满了、飘香着、

Classics Absurdity

Expiation on Spring and Autumn
A New Account of The Tales of The World
Spreading like a big feast
Confucian Analects

Laotze Zhuang Zi Confucius Mencius
Mo-tse Xun Zi Lie Zi Sun Zi
Eight sages sing together
Rhythmic melodious

Still there are Guigu Zi and Hanfei Zi
Gongsunlong Zi and Huannan Zi
On the ferry lost to the scenery
Yan Zi knew not the hour
Forgot the Lv's Commentaries of History
Absent for long

Milky Way
All birds dance together
In the courtyard on the table
Are piled with ink scented

诗经、太平经、山海经
坛经、三字经
经经奇妙、句句江海

远处、树下、亭台阁
包装着、摆列着
国语、左传、楚辞、宋论
五颜六色、光彩夺目
闲情偶寄、古文观止
字字入骨、语语生香

贞观政要
阅微草堂笔记
商讨战国策
回忆搜神记
传言文心雕龙
齐学弟子规
人声鼎沸、热闹非凡

吕氏大谈着春秋
孙子宽论着家语
颜氏弘扬着家训
新书、新序、法言
百花齐放、百家争鸣

The Book of Songs The Scripture of the Great Peace
Mountains and Rivers
Altar Sutra Three Character Primer
Every book superior each sentence profound

In the distance under the trees in the pavilion
Packed displayed
History of Different Kingdoms History of Spring and Autumn Period
The Songs of Chu Commentaries on Song
Colorful splendid

Critics On Plays China's Ancient Prose classical view
Every word deep each phrase lifelike

Remonstration during the period of Zhen Guan
Yuewei Caotang Notes
Discuss Strategies of the Warring States
Recall the Record of Ghost Stories
Talk of Wen Xin Diao Long/ Historiography
Learn about Di Zi Gui
The babble of voices sound like bubbles of boiling water in the jar

Lv was talking about The Spring and Autumn Annal

忽然传报、礼到
周礼、仪礼
中庸、大学、尚书随行
黄帝大乐、开怀痛饮
从此学会了内经

宴散、礼毕
众人离席
庭院又恢复了平静
嫦娥隐隐睡去、山尖
露出了缕缕阳光

2014 年秋

Confucius was remarking on Confucius Sayings
Yan was promoting his Family Instructions
Jiayi's New Book Liu Xiang's New Order Yang Xiong's Standards
A hundred kinds of flowers are in bloom
A hundred schools of thought contend

Word came that
The Rites of Zhou The Ceremonies And Rites
The Doctrine of Mean The Great Learning The Classic Of History
Followed
Yellow Emperor was joyful
Drank to his heart's content
From which he learned Inner Canon /Canon of Medicine

Feast ended rites completed
Everyone left
The courtyard regained its quietness
Change fell asleep over the mountain
Dawn is starting to show

Autumn 2014

谁，偷走了你的灵魂

谁，偷走了你的灵魂
剩下空荡荡的躯壳
四处游荡
随波逐浪
碧海孤舟

谁，偷走了你的灵魂
剩下红唇洁齿
李代桃僵
丢失了方向
荒废了理想
人云亦云
大同小异

谁，偷走了你的灵魂
埋葬了欢笑
淹没了激情
呆如木鸡
胆小如泥

谁，偷走了你的灵魂

Who Has Stolen Your Soul

Who Has Stolen Your Soul
Leaving the empty shell
Wandering about
Floating with the wave
A lonely sail on the sea

Who has stolen your soul
Leaving red lips and white teeth
Plum tree sacrificed itself for peach tree
Lost direction
Wasted ideal
Echoed the views of others
General resemblance with minor differences

Who has stolen your soul
Buried laughter
Drowned passion
Dumb as a wooden chicken
As timid as a mouse

Who has stolen your soul

眼睁睁，望着错过的美女
轻盈的脚步
眼睁睁，听着模糊的知己
缠绵的记忆
点点滴滴
欲言又止
声声叹息

谁，偷走了你的灵魂
以至平淡无奇
以至一片空虚
以至乱想胡思
以至酒醉金迷

谁，偷走了你的灵魂
以至空空如洗
以至朝忙晚碌
以至不苟言笑
以至满脸横肌

谁，偷走了你的灵魂
且欠刻骨铭心
且欠欢天喜地
且欠童叟无欺

Watch helplessly the pretty girl you missed
Walking by with light steps
Listen helplessly the self you ignored
Becoming fond memories
Bit by bit
Want to speak but hesitate
Sigh after sigh

Who has stolen your soul
So that you are dull and plain
Void and empty
Think and fancy
Drunk and sunk

Who has stolen your soul
So that you are poor as robbed of
Busy as a bee
Serious in speech and manner
Face muscles horizontal

Who has stolen your soul
Lacking in bone engraved and heart imprinted
Joy and delight
Equal honesty with the old and the young

谁，偷走了你的灵魂
颠沛流离
希望
及早归还
不曾丢失
斑斓耀眼
生生世世
永恒不息

2014 年秋夜

Who has stolen your soul

Leaving you displaced

Hoping to return soon

Or never lost

Glittering and dazzling

Life after life

Eternal

Autumn night 2014

惊魂古梦

很久很久
以前的楼兰古国
有三个
俊秀的楚国王子
他们有三个
共同的爱好
吟诗、品酒、弄弦
并且他们同时
爱上了三个
秀丽的晋国公主

有一天
三个王子与三个公主
在一片辽阔的草原上
同时大喊三声
我爱你
我爱你
我爱你

忽然间
电闪雷鸣

Blood-Freezing Old Dream

Years ago
There lived in Ancient Kroraina
Three handsome princes of Chu
All of whom
Shared the same hobbies
Chanting poems   tasting wine   playing music
Meanwhile
They fell in love with three pretty princesses of Jin

One day
They met on a vast pasture
Shouting aloud three times
I love you
I love you
I love you

All of a sudden
Storm came
With lightning and thunders
Shaking the earth

狂风暴雨
地动山摇

干涸的河流灌满了
灼热的泉水
汹涌澎湃
光彩夺目
涛声四起
雷霆万钧

过了好一阵
忽然、又
万籁俱寂
鸦雀无声
吱吱吱
传来轻盈的脚步
婀娜的声音

啊！
举目横扫
来者何人？
答曰
“小女子、无形是也”

即时

Dried rivers are filled

Hot spring water

Rolling and surging

Eye catching   breath taking

Roaring roaming

Crushing   devastating

Quite a long time

Everything fell into silence

Neither crow nor sparrow could be heart

Then there came

The squeaks of light steps

Elegant

Ah

Looking around

Who is it

A voice replied

Miss Invisible

Instantly

The crowd became quiet

All flowers faded

Both the sky and the earth soudless

群人无语
万花无色
天地无音
无喜无怒

舒畅无比
心如醉酒
身如飞仙
如梦如痴

醉矣！
醉矣！

2014 年秋夜

Neither joy nor sorrow

Joy filled
Heart drunken
Body slight as fairy
Dreamy   obsessed

Drunk
Totally

Autumn night of 2014

电　影

迷茫的小道
缥缈的亭台
婀娜的舞姿
霸王怒吼着

李白踱步着丛林
刘伶醉酒着郊野
曹操赤脚着迎宾
庄子谈着逍遥游

牛郎寻找着织女
梁山伯挽扶着祝英台
贾宝玉凝望着林黛玉
罗密欧吻别着朱丽叶

一张张美丽的脸孔
一片片肥沃的土地
一个个纠结的朝代
一对对悲情的男女

梦、醒了又醉

Movie

Hazy path
Airy pavilion
Graceful dancing figures
Xiang Yu the conqueror stormed
Li Bai the poet strolled in the woods
Liu Lun got drunk in the wild fields
Cao Cao welcomed his guests bare footed
Zhuang Zi talked about Peripateticism

Cowboy is looking for Weaving Girl
Liang Shanbo is supporting Zhu Yingtai
Jia Bayou is gazing at Lin Daiyu
Romeo is kissing Juliet goodbye

One pretty face after another
One fertile land after another
One arcane dynasty after another
One sobbing couple after another

Dream awake and drunk
Wine emptied and refilled

酒、干了又满
人、散了又聚
心、碎了又合

原来
电影是心的模样
随心所欲
无拘无束

原来
电影是爱的温床
男欢女爱
各种各样

原来
电影是犯罪的天堂
战争杀戮
草芥人命

原来
电影是生活的魔兽
张牙舞爪
怒吼雷鸣

电影

People dispersed and reunited
Heart broken and recovered

Movie is
Shaped like a heart
Follow your heart
Unrestrained

Movie is
The warm bed of love
Between man and woman
Various

Movie is
Paradise for crime
Fighting and killing
Treating humans as worthless as grass

Movie is
Monster of likfe
Baring fangs and opening claws
Roaring like thunders

Movie is
Player of your heart's voice

是你心灵的播放器
电影
是你梦寐的展示厅
电影
是你蜜糖的生产基地
电影
是你与情人苟合的无人区

电影、而且
是迷魂的妖精
是脚步的召集号
是眼泪的收购站
是幸福与悲哀的终结者

原来
电影

是你自己
书写自己
观看自己
感动自己

新的生活
旧的理想
粘合在一起

Movie is

Showroom of you dream

Movie is

Production base of honey

Movie is

Depopulated zone where you have sex with your lover

Movie is also

Bewildering elf

Siren for marching on

Recycling center for tears

Terminator of happiness and sorrow

Movie

Is

You

Writing about yourself

Watching yourself

Moving yourself

New life

Old ideal

Patched together

一切

重新开始

2014 年秋

Everything

Start again

Autumn 2014

枷　锁

猛烈的阳光
怒烤着大地
茂盛的大树、低沉的小草
还有、那娇艳孔雀
凶残的猎豹、斑驳的花虎
无一、都不敢吱声

那高高矮矮大大小小
的人们
肥肥瘦瘦黑黑白白着
满脸横肉、故张声势
半驼的峰背
却配个狰狞的面孔
那小孩、婴儿的襁褓里
声音也异常尖利

枷锁
那透明的枷锁
锁住了脚步
荒废了年华
锁住了笑容
迷失了方向

Chains

Strong sunlight
Beating on the land
Leafy trees　low grass
And the dainty peacock
The cruel cheetah　the variegated tiger
All remain silent

Tall or short　old or young
People
Fat or thin　dark or fair
Ugly looking　swashbuckling
Half humpbacked
With a savage look
Even a baby in the cradle
Cries in a high pitched voice

Chains
Transparent
Bounded the steps
Neglected prime years
Locked smiling faces
Lost the direction

以道德的楞子
没有道德
以长辈的形象
不知廉耻
以文字的铁索
脑满肠肥
以消沉的思维
自圆其说

甚至
以七彩的花纹
以深红的美酒
以婀娜的身姿
以耀眼的舞台

枷锁
那无形的枷锁
锁住了一切
行尸走肉
人云亦云
道听途说
故弄玄虚

枷锁
那害人的枷锁
消磨了意志

Example of morals

Does immoral deeds

Image of honor

Knows no sense of shame

Literary icon

Enjoys life heavy jowled and potbellied

Under the cloak of a thinker

Justifies himself

Even in the form of

Colorful strips

Deep red wine

Slim figure

Eye-catching state

Chains

Invisible chains

Locked everything

A walking corpse and running flesh

Talking like a parrot

Relying on hearsay

Bluffing kick up a cloud of dust

Chains

Harmful chains

Wore down the will

削减了欢乐
销毁了爱情
浪费了生命

硝烟弥漫
却又无声无影

寻觅吧
那钥匙
宝藏的钥匙
金光闪闪
所向披靡
乘风破浪
色彩斑斓

寻觅吧
那钥匙
思想的钥匙
在蔚蓝的大海里
在巍巍的峻岭上
在熙熙攘攘的人潮中
在日夜奔腾的牛群里
在重重叠叠的书页里
在孔庙里、在诗经中
在金灿灿的稻田里
在香甜甜的果园中

Ruined the pleasure
Destroyed love
Wasted life

A cloud of smoke floated
Soundless shadeless

Just look
For the key
The key to the treasure
Golden
Carry the world before one
Ride the wind and waves
Hopeful colorful

Just look
For the key
The key to thought
In the blue sea
Over high mountain
Among the bustling crowd
Amid the surging cattle herd
Between the overlapping /overlaying pages
In Confucius temple in the Book of Poetry
In golden rich fields
In sweet scented orchard

寻觅吧
那钥匙
梦寐以求的钥匙
愿昂首挺胸
愿无所顾忌
愿笑容可掬

愿
无忧无虑
无惊无险
无我无他
无怨无悔

愿
不枉此生
宁静安祥

愿
人间盛宴
千古流长

2014 年秋
有感于放开思维
摆脱束缚的欣喜

Just look

For the key

The dream key/key in your dream

Wishing to walk with chin up and chest out

Having nothing to fear

Radiate with smiles

Wishing

No worries or troubles

No risks or accidents

Neither others nor myself

No regrets or repentance/rue or regrets

Wishing

Not to live an idle life

But one with peace

Wishing

The grand feast of the world

Would last long

Autumn of 2014

From pleasure of opening the mind

Free from chains

梦

麻绳
就是梦

Dream

Dream

Is rope of hemp

笑与泪

夜色
迷人般的黑暗
诱惑欲望的魂体
朦胧中旋行
摸爬滚打、喧嚣

前行的尽头
是一串串纠结的泪珠
泪珠的晶莹
洗浴出一片深邃
深邃散去、溪湖般的
柔弱、软化
飘逸着淋漓苦涩

一滴一滴
一片一片
汇聚出一辽浩瀚的大海
大海般的孤怜
强大的弱者

白日的欢颜
对角的笑靥

Laughter And Tears

Night view
Inviting darkness
Luring the body with desire
Traveling in the mist
Tumbling rolling bustling

End of the road
Hang strings of teardrops
Sparkling
In the depth
When the darkness fades
Tender and lake-like softness
Appear painful

One drop after another
One piece after another
Join and form a boundless sea
Pitiful as the sea
A powerful weakness

Smile in the day
Angular dimples

模具般的狂喜
流转、迷茫
喜悦出一架僵硬
僵化的背后
是一汪泪波涟漪的清泉

一个个
一顶顶
笑脸相迎
面面相觑

一出出
一段段
好戏连台
爱恨交加

泪水腐蚀着笑脸
融化成一堆泡影
泡沫的飞溅
飞奔出罪恶的根源

笑与泪
纠缠不清
泪与笑
永不凋零

2015 年春

Modeled ecstasy

Turning lost

A skeleton of joy

Behind the stiffness

A spring of rippled tears

One by one

Head by head

Give a welcoming look

Exchange doubtful glances

One act after another

One scene after another

A series of good plays

Hatred mingled with love

Tears rust the smiling faces

All melt into bubbles

Foams splash

And sparkle into the source of the evil

Laughter and tears

Always mingled

Tears and laughter

Never withered

Spring 2015

超　人

人便是人
为何要装超人

路

路本无路
行走是路

爱　情

由它去吧
爱来便来
爱去便去

Superman

Human is man

Why pretend to be superman

Road

Road itself doesn't exist

Walking makes road

Love

Let it be

Come it may

Go it may

世　界

说小就小
说大就大

金　钱

有时装无
无时装有
悟时无装

美　女

初见有效
再见成效
常见无效

World

Small while small

Big while big

Money

Pretend to be poor when rich

Pretend to rich when poor

No pretending when understanding

Beauty

Pretty at first sight

Less pretty at second sight

Not pretty at a hundredth sight

朋　友

常来是朋
常帮是友

夜　色

是黑的

计　划

比现实假

知　音

往往无音

Friend

Frequent coming is friendly

Frequent help is friend

Night View

Dark

Plan

False

Compared with reality

Soulmate

A silent soul at your side

纠 结

是借口

忙

是对的

孤 独

睡吧
无人知道

风 光

是风景
会凋谢的

Dilemma

An excuse

Busy

Alright

Solitude

Just sleep

Nobody knows

Sight

Scenic view

That will fade

傲　气

最好
藏点

情　人

说吧

怒　火

烧不尽
见恶就生

贫　民

谁说的？

Arrogance

Better

Hide

Lover

Just say it

Flames of Fury

Never burn out

Burn up at the sight of evil

Poor People

Who pours out that

大 学

读吧
否则爸爸会骂

风 筝

飞吧
白费心机

教 师

是好人

豪 车

买来期待
买后无奈

College

Just go to
Or Dad will blame you

Kite

Just fly
All plans are in vain

Teachers

Good people

Expensive Car

Hopeful before purchase
Helpless after purchase

豪　宅

屋比人大
心比屋大
睡前游荡
睡后一样

尘　埃

山的爸爸

花

让人折磨

Grand House

House bigger than the person

Heart bigger than the house

Wander about before sleep

All the same when sleep

Dust

The forefather

Of mountain

Flower

Torture man

And wait for torture

蛇

弯的

酒

喝吧
最好不是水

累

心的事

高血压

太兴奋了

Snake

Bent

Wine

Just drink

Better not water

Fatigue

Matter of the heart

High Blood Pressure

Much too high

静

才是高手

思

考吧

文　化

对的

科　学

科科来好
样样属实

Serenity

Is superior

Thinking

Questioning

Culture

Correct

Science

Subjects true
Objects real

成　绩

写上便可

恋　爱

男女的事

钱

好吧

国　家

我爱祖国
也爱家乡

Score

Just write it down

Falling In Love

Is between man and woman

Money

It is fine.

Country

I love my motherland

And homeland as well

商　品

商店的物品

兑　现

成交吧

夫　妻

是一对

同　学

来吧

Goods

Things in the stores

Exchange For Cash

It's a deal

Husband and Wife

A couple

Classmate

Just come

女朋友

也是人

风　流

随风流走

广　告

身外之词
不在心里

熬　夜

煮吧
会熟的

Girlfriend

Also human

Romance And Elegance

Gone with the wind

Ad

Words beside the body
Outside the heart

Stay Up

Just do it
And it will be done

贵　贱

用来比较的

大

小的敌人

高

因为我们都矮

胖　子

能写诗？

Superior or Inferior

Nothing but comparative

The Big

Enemy of the small

Tall

As we are all short

Fatty

Can he write poems?

马　路

走马的

穷

富的表亲

富

慢点

灯

点上
光来了

Road

Is to tread on

Poverty

The cousin of wealth

Wealth

Slow down

Lamp

Light up
Light comes

床

睡吧

短

正好

长

吓人

海

水的兄弟
开会来了

Bed

Just sleep on

Short

Just long enough

Long

Too scary

The Sea

The brothers of water

Come for meeting

水

湿的
一旦变硬
成冰了

笑

哭吧
不得

哭

口大了

诗

好东西

Water

Wet

Turns into ice

When hardened

Laugh

If you can not

Cry

Cry

With mouth wide open

Poems

Precious

词

用来填的

好

同意

坏

反对

Lyrics

To fill

Into music

Yes

Agree

No

Opposed